Chief Stoick was a proud leader. He did everything the Viking way. But sometimes the Viking way was the hard way.

His son, Hiccup, knew another way.
It was the dragon way. Dragons could
help make life easier.

Hiccup convinced Stoick to learn how
to fly a dragon.

Hiccup and his dragon, Toothless, offered to teach Stoick to ride and Stoick was eager to learn.

"Whoa, Dad," Hiccup said. "Before you ride, you have to show the dragon he can trust you."

Hiccup placed Stoick's hand on
Toothless' snout.

Toothless closed his eyes and lowered
his head. It was a sign of trust.

Stoick was eager for the next lesson.
He jumped onto Toothless' back and
took off into the sky.

Hiccup warned Stoick to go slowly. But he didn't listen.

Hiccup frowned. His dad had a lot to learn.

The next morning, Hiccup couldn't find Toothless. He looked all over for him.

At last, Stoick appeared, riding Toothless.

Stoick was excited. "We've been all over the village," Stoick said. "With Toothless, being chief has never been so easy!"

"But, Dad," Hiccup said, "Toothless is my dragon. You can't just take him."

Stoick looked thoughtful. "All right, so find me a dragon of my own," Stoick replied.

Hiccup took Stoick to the Dragon Training
Academy. Hiccup's friends were eager to
help the chief pick a dragon.

Snotlout brought out Hookfang. "He is a Monstrous Nightmare, the only dragon strong enough for big men like us," he told the chief.

Next, Astrid showed off her dragon, Stormfly. "Just because she is beautiful, it doesn't mean she's not tough," Astrid said.

Finally, Fishlegs introduced his dragon,
Meatlug. "How could you not love
a Gronckle?" he asked Stoick.

Stoick liked all the dragons. But he couldn't find one he liked as much as Toothless.

Suddenly, a message arrived for Chief Stoick. It said that one of his fishing boats was in trouble!

Stoick and Hiccup hopped onto Toothless' back and flew to the rescue!

The fishing boat was under attack
by a Thunderdrum dragon.

He was stealing the Vikings' fish!

Stoick fought the Thunderdrum and captured him. He was very impressed by the dragon's strength.

"This is the one, Hiccup! I've found my dragon!" Stoick said.

Stoick brought the Thunderdrum back to the Dragon Training Academy. Then he asked Hiccup to help train his new dragon.

"Be gentle, Dad. Remember, he has to trust you," Hiccup said.

But Stoick didn't listen. He and the Thunderdrum fought and fought . . .

. . . until the Thunderdrum escaped!

Stoick and Hiccup tracked the dragon to a cave far away. Another dragon was there too.

There, they discovered that the Thunderdrum had a secret. The dragon's friend was hurt!

"He's trying to help his friend!" Stoick said. "That's why he took our fish!"

Stoick sent Hiccup to get help for the
wounded dragon.

As soon as Hiccup left, a pack of wild
boars charged the cave! It was up to
Stoick and the Thunderdrum to fight them.

Stoick gently placed his hand on the Thunderdrum's snout. "I want to help. Trust me," he told the dragon.

The Thunderdrum closed his eyes and lowered his head. Again, it was a sign of trust.

Stoick took off the dragon's muzzle,
then climbed onto its back.

They fought the wild boars as a team!
And they won!

Later, Hiccup returned with help for the wounded dragon.

By that time, Stoick and the Thunderdrum were old friends. "Look at us, we've bonded," Stoick said.

Hiccup smiled. His dad had just learned an important lesson.

The Viking way could also be the
dragon way.